i am neurotic

i am neurotic

neurotic

(and so are you)

Lianna Kong

with photos by
Matthew Stacey

harperstudio
An Imprint of HarperCollins*Publishers*

HarperCollins books may be purchased for educational, business,
or sales promotional use. For information please write: Special
Markets Department, HarperCollins Publishers, 10 East 53rd Street,
New York, NY 10022.

For more information about this book or other books from
HarperStudio, visit www.theharperstudio.com.

FIRST EDITION

Designed by Eric Butler

ISBN 978-0-06-179147-5

09 10 11 12 13   ID/RRD   10 9 8 7 6 5 4 3 2 1

contents

intro

duction

■ There are certain moments in life when, in an unflinching moment of self-awareness, we have a "come-to-Jesus" experience and recognize deep emotional truths about ourselves. Mine came in an office bathroom. Everything was going just splendidly: tights at my ankles, toilet paper perfectly blanketing the seat, the reassuring aroma of disinfecting industrial cleaner, and two Diet Cokes and one Starbucks venti vanilla latte ready to go. "Go" being the operative word here. All I wanted to do was pee—I had the means and the motive. And yet, there was one tiny problem. How could I possibly pee with my coworker sitting right next to me doing her business? The deafening sound of urine splashing on porcelain paralyzed my excretory system. My bladder, apparently incapable of functioning in the presence of others, waited impatiently for the person next door to finish and vacate the bathroom. Even after my coworker left, I had to mentally coax my bladder to do the job it was designed to do. Good-bye normal, hello neurotic.

Upon reflection, it occurred to me that this was not an isolated incident. I recognized a distinct pattern to my urinary behavior. I was consciously and purposely choosing to use the bathroom between 10:00 and 11:00 a.m. or 3:00 and 4:00 p.m. These were the only times peeing was allowed. No matter how much I had to urinate, no matter how urgent bathroom breaks were, they were done on the schedule or not at all. At 4:15, it was a long, long ride home.

introduction

Somehow I had deduced the optimal bathroom break times for myself: when no one would be present and I could pee in solitude and silence. For this I earned a gold star. When people encroach on my private bathroom time, I feel annoyed and must wait patiently for that person to leave before I can finish my business. I do not do well on road trips.

Thankfully, I am not alone. The night before, my best friend called to discuss how much she detested touching cotton balls and was trying to find an alternative method to remove the nail polish from her toes. Every morning during my commute, I watch a germophobic man tug at the cuffs of his shirtsleeves, trying desperately to pull them over his hands so he can hold onto the railing without having to touch it. Another friend's movie-going habits were revealed when a last-minute candy run to CVS caused us to miss the previews and she adamantly refused to enter the theater. Apparently, missing the previews diminished the pleasure of the movie-watching experience. Our dinner-and-a-movie outing quickly turned into a dinner-only affair, leaving me ample time to stop at a local bar to drink away my lament over how neuroses can sometimes get in the way of life.

The seed of the idea was planted in my brain. It was only a matter of taking advantage of the Internet's robust selection of free blogging applications and on April 29, 2008, after a couple of hours' mental labor, www.iamneurotic.com was birthed into the Internet. My mission was clear: to create an entertaining procrastination tool in the form of a blog and provide a space where my friends and I could anonymously confess our neuroses after it became obvious that sending out mass e-mails about our neurotic tendencies was only hurting our relationships. It turns out a lot of people wanted to read about our neuroses. Not only that, they wanted to comment on our neuroses and share their own. As the submissions poured in, it occurred to me that perhaps the blog was acting as a sort of social salve allowing people to unburden themselves from the weight of their often hidden neuroses. I felt honored and more than happy to help them take the weight off their shoulders.

The term *neurotic* is not an official behavioral health diagnosis. It can't be found in the *DSM* (*Diagnostic and Statistical Manual of Mental Disorders*), and you won't score yourself any sweet drugs for being neurotic. It's more of a colloquial term to describe a variety of disorders or idiosyncrasies. Often it's used to describe a personality type. Woody Allen, Larry David, and Monica Geller from *Friends* are people who have come to embody and represent neurotic behavior in popular culture. We often refer to them or use them as examples of neurotic behavior. This kind of circular-firing-squad logic is less than useful when attempting to mollify the Internet critics who argue that the postings on my site aren't really neuroses at all. Truthfully, I found myself allowing the content of the submissions to guide my already loose interpretation of the term.

Either way, www.iamneurotic.com was never designed to be a dictionary of neuroses. Rather it is an attempt to provide a space where people can feel connected to a community of people like themselves—people who are aware their behavior isn't quite normal but who nevertheless don't want to think of themselves as "nucking futs." It is both compelling and validating

introduction

to realize how many people share the same rituals, paranoias, and aversions. I am comforted by the number of submissions I received from people who feel the same way I do about bathrooms. Guiltily, I feel a little more normal knowing that people have far more extreme neuroses, and yet I often find myself quite defensive when people deride a submission as totally crazy. These are my people now—and we all bleed red. Only difference is, we rush to clean it up with six different brands of household cleaning agents. The i am neurotic website gives us a chance to laugh at our own ridiculousness, but not a license to ridicule one another.

This book contains a collection of neuroses that were submitted to the site over the past year. For fellow neurotics, I'm sure you understand that what makes perfect sense to the logic of your mind rarely makes sense to others. For those of you in denial, I hope this book shows you how neurotic you really are and that you just haven't realized it. When I started the site, I had the privilege of being let in on some of the more quirky and intimate aspects of the human psyche. I hope that in looking through this book, you derive at least some combination of the shock, humor, wry affection, and camaraderie I experienced. At the same time, I hope you'll start to understand how incredibly intimate and defining these neuroses can be and why people have tried so hard to hide them . . . until now.

Lianna Kong

i am neurotic

1.

putting the A in anal:
settle
for
nothing
less
than
obsessive

I am very picky about my chocolate chip cookies. I'll separate the batter into forty-eight tablespoon balls, and then add twelve chocolate chips to each ball. They are much tastier with the perfect number of chocolate chips.

Toilet paper must be on the roll with the loose end trailing over the top not the bottom. I have been compelled to fix this error in friends' homes, churches, and public restrooms. I feel a nagging urgency for the rest of the day if I know about a wrong-facing toilet paper roll.

Stacks of papers always have to be perfectly in line. If I see one sheet partially sticking out, I will stop whatever I'm doing and reshuffle the stack so that it's perfectly rectangular again.

Food on my plate cannot touch other
food. Any part that has touched has to
be placed to the side on the plate and
not eaten. I consider it contaminated.

Whenever I open a new pack of cigarettes I absolutely must take the third cigarette from the right on the front row and flip it upside down. This is the lucky cigarette, and it must be smoked last. If I forget to flip it, I get all nervous until I open the next pack.

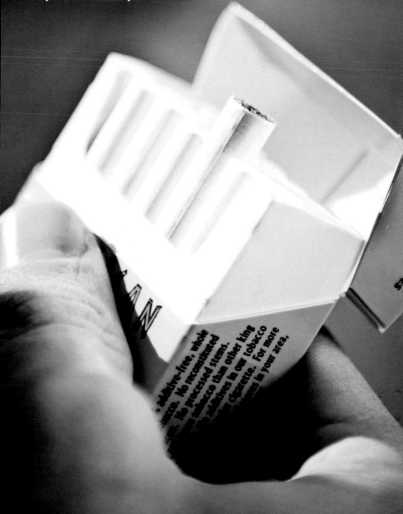

I always make sure I order loose coins in a single vertical column according to size (largest on the bottom, smallest on the top) and all facing heads down. If this is not done correctly it will bother me until it is completed.

I have precisely twenty nuts every morning before 11:00. These are counted out of the packet individually using a homemade cardboard nut counter, which consists of five rows of four equally marked-out squares.

Before I go to sleep at night I must make sure that the sheets are tucked in just right. The bedspread can't be wrinkled, and it must all be perfectly even before I get into bed. I even wait until my girlfriend's asleep and then fix the sheets with her in the bed. I know when I wake up the sheets will be strewn about, but at least I can go to sleep knowing that the blankets are nicely tucked.

Whenever I go to the bottled water cooler at work I always have to take the cup second from the top of the dispenser in case the first one has been touched by someone else.

In elementary school my friends and I would pass notes on a single sheet of paper. I would always send it back with my note, but I would also correct my friends' spelling and grammar with a red pen.

If I see a telephone cord all tangled up, I have to stop and fix it, no matter how long it takes. I am so glad that cell phones are becoming more common.

Ever since I learned how to solve Rubik's Cube I can't leave one unsolved. Sometimes others will play around with my Rubik's Cube; once it's messed up, I don't have a choice—I have to fix it.

I always have to
staple my papers
together three times.
I feel that if I don't do this,
the staple will fall off and
my papers will separate;
but this way, if one staple
falls out I still have two more
to hold the papers together.

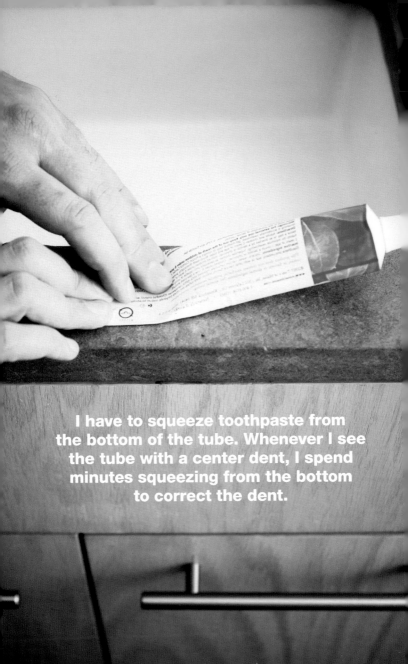

I have to squeeze toothpaste from the bottom of the tube. Whenever I see the tube with a center dent, I spend minutes squeezing from the bottom to correct the dent.

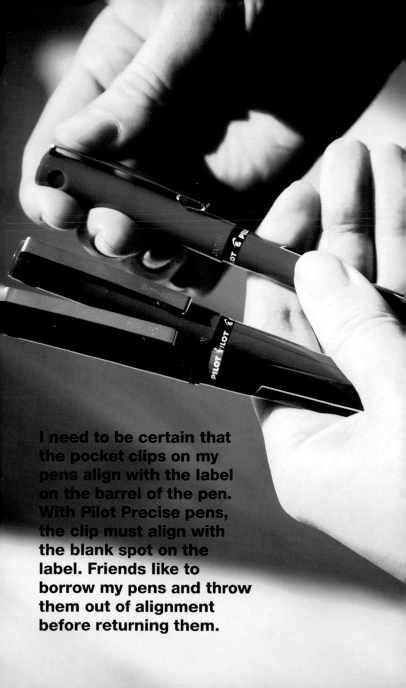

I need to be certain that the pocket clips on my pens align with the label on the barrel of the pen. With Pilot Precise pens, the clip must align with the blank spot on the label. Friends like to borrow my pens and throw them out of alignment before returning them.

When I'm loading my groceries onto
the conveyor at the supermarket
all UPC codes must be facing the
cashier in their proper orientation.

30.00
6.872

price per gallon includes taxes

E85 Ethanol

$3.459

I have a thing about numbers that end in zero. When I'm pumping gas, if it stops at $38.46, I have to get it to $39.00 even. If it's $39.01, I have to pump more to get it to $40.00. I may spend more money, but at least the numbers are even.

Push Here
To
Start

ALL

2.

can't touch this:
no—
seriously,
you
can't
touch
this

I cannot touch cotton balls. The feel of raw cotton makes me grind my teeth, cringe, and shudder, while those around me judge my lunacy. It really is almost a handicap.

I hate the feel of unpolished wood. Holding a Popsicle stick gives me goose bumps. I have to eat Popsicles by holding the stick with my sleeve, even though this gives me purple stains.

I can't stand multiple bumps
close together: corn on the cob,
multiple pimples, popcorn ceilings—
anything with multiple bumps.
They seriously freak me out.

Crumbs in butter tubs or jars of jelly drive me crazy. I have perfected my spreading abilities to ensure that I never transplant crumbs into containers. When I lived with many room-mates, I would write "No Crumbs" on the lid of the butter container.

I have an intense repulsion for sponges and refuse to use utensils that have been washed with a sponge. I typically carry plastic utensils with me to use in case machine-washed items are not available, or I rewash the items using just my hands and water.

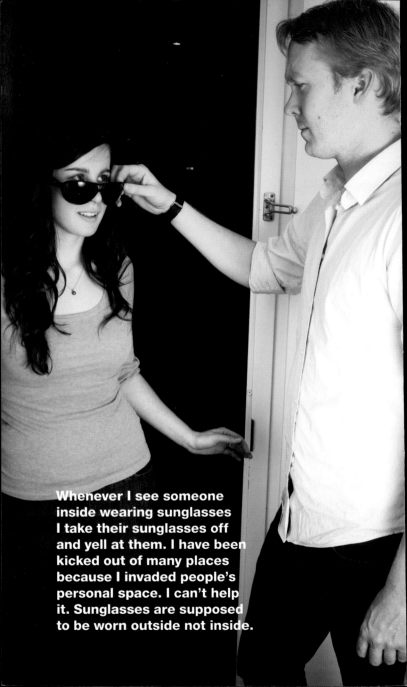

Whenever I see someone inside wearing sunglasses I take their sunglasses off and yell at them. I have been kicked out of many places because I invaded people's personal space. I can't help it. Sunglasses are supposed to be worn outside not inside.

I can't eat both ends of my French fries. I don't know why. I will stare at my basket of fries and try to decide which end I want to eat (usually the one that's not crusty or dark brown or wonky). I eat the fry up to the tip, and then throw it back into the basket.

I find it nearly impossible to wear any shoes other than flip-flops and socks, and I have to cut a slash in between the big toe and middle toe area of each sock so the tongue will fit.

I can only eat the middle of foods, like chips, eggs, or sandwiches. I leave all the crusts in a perfect form so they make up the shape again. My mates hate me for this at dinners.

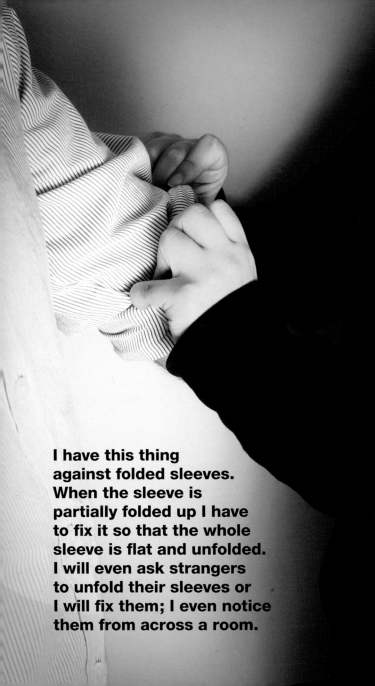

I have this thing
against folded sleeves.
When the sleeve is
partially folded up I have
to fix it so that the whole
sleeve is flat and unfolded.
I will even ask strangers
to unfold their sleeves or
I will fix them; I even notice
them from across a room.

I cannot look at or touch my belly button. I cannot have anyone else touch my belly. The thought of being touched makes me keel over with my arms wrapped around my belly, concealing my belly button.

My girlfriend cannot have sex with her socks on, especially if there is only one on. She says that her mind won't be able to focus on anything else when they're on.

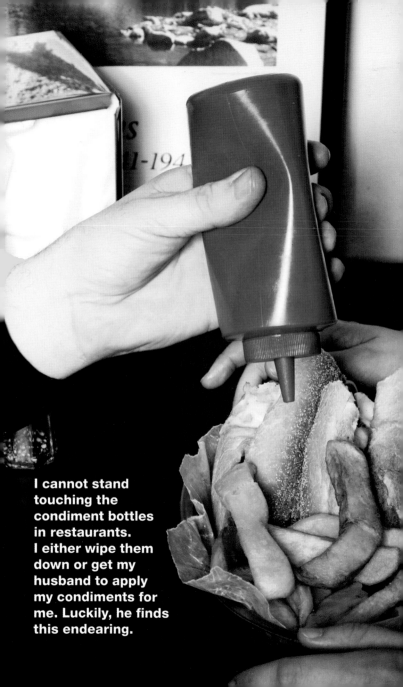

I cannot stand touching the condiment bottles in restaurants. I either wipe them down or get my husband to apply my condiments for me. Luckily, he finds this endearing.

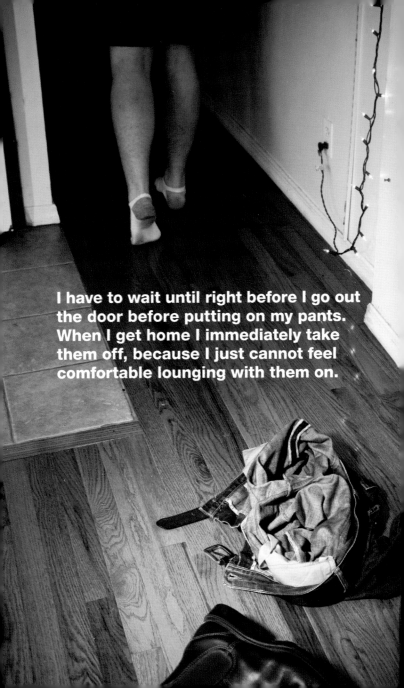

I have to wait until right before I go out the door before putting on my pants. When I get home I immediately take them off, because I just cannot feel comfortable lounging with them on.

The seam on a paper coffee cup can never be in the lid opening or sip hole. The feeling of the seam on my lip drives me nuts, and I'm afraid it will increase the chance of coffee spilling down my shirt.

I get an extreme feeling of disgust every time I ride the subway. I can't get rid of it until I wash the bottom of my shoes and put my clothes in the wash. I also have to wash my hands, and encourage others around me to do the same.

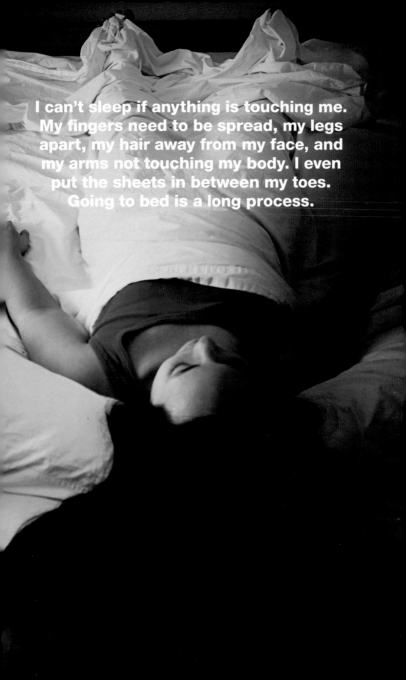

I can't sleep if anything is touching me. My fingers need to be spread, my legs apart, my hair away from my face, and my arms not touching my body. I even put the sheets in between my toes. Going to bed is a long process.

3.

it's not you, it's me:
how to have an awkward interaction

Each day I have to touch someone I do not know, with a quick pat on the shoulder or a tap on the back. Some days I get in my car telling myself I want fast food, but actually I just have the urge to lightly tap a stranger.

I have an imaginary keyboard on my hands, which is mostly on my thumbs, but the space bar is the side of my pointer finger. When I am anxious or stressed I will fixate on one particular word and type it on my fake keyboard over and over again. Friends can sometimes even guess the word.

Whenever I kiss my girlfriend
I have a need to push my glasses up
using her nose.

My pens must remain untouched by other human hands. I will happily let someone use my pen, but I let the borrower keep it or it goes straight in the garbage. It's not a germ or hygiene issue, but some deep violation of the symbiotic relationship between one and one's pen.

I can't stop myself from aligning the strings on my hooded sweatshirts, and even try to fix other people's strings. They drive me absolutely nuts.

If I see the tag of a shirt
sticking out I have to go fix it.
This is sometimes awkward,
but I can't stand to see it.

Whenever I am walking and listening to music I pretend I am the star of a music video and start lip-synching. If I see others noticing me, I put my head down and pretend I don't see them.

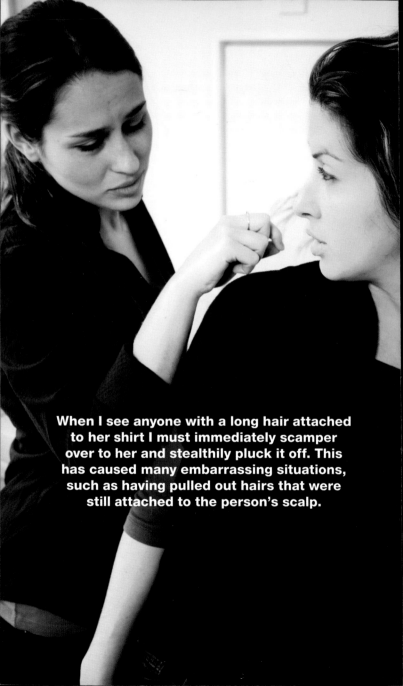

When I see anyone with a long hair attached to her shirt I must immediately scamper over to her and stealthily pluck it off. This has caused many embarrassing situations, such as having pulled out hairs that were still attached to the person's scalp.

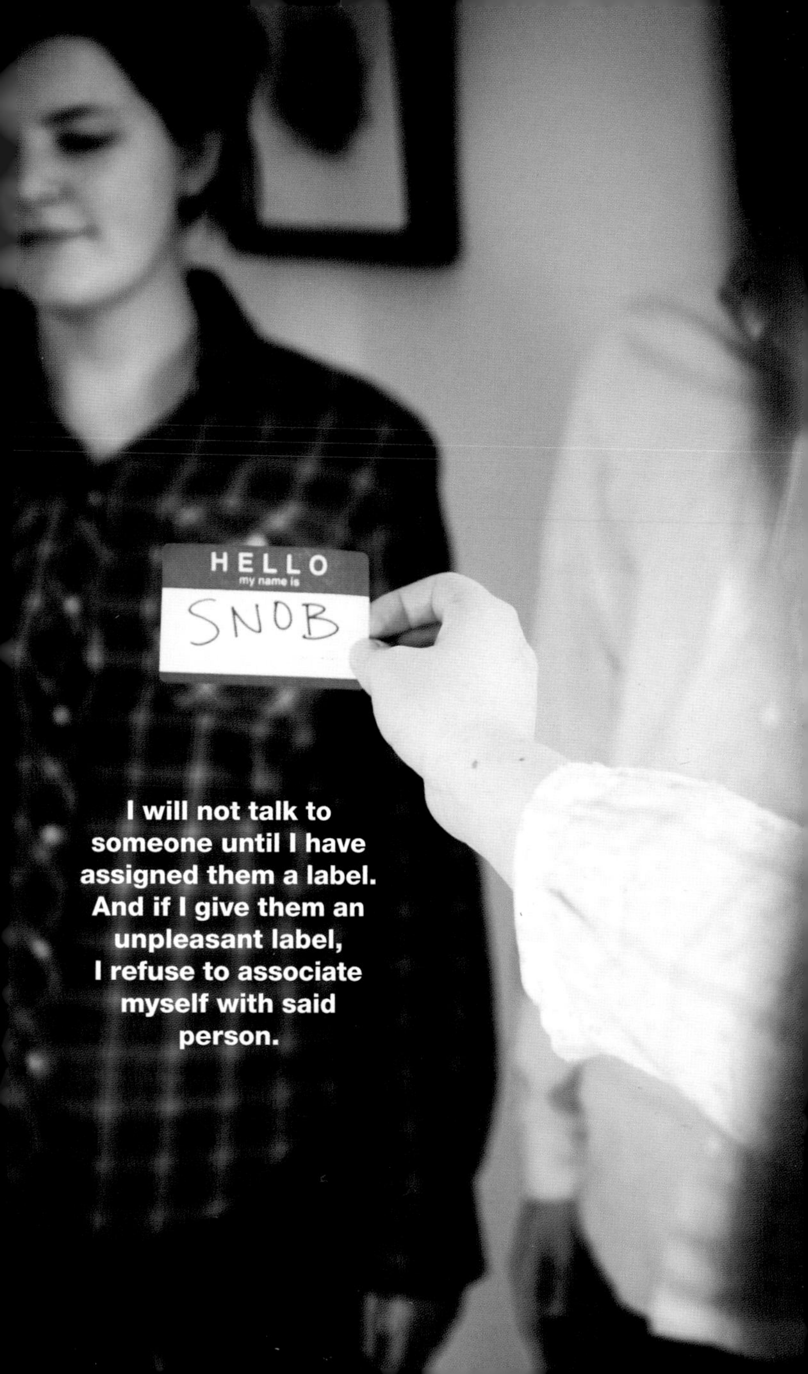

HELLO
my name is
SNOB

I will not talk to someone until I have assigned them a label. And if I give them an unpleasant label, I refuse to associate myself with said person.

When I'm crossing the street and there are a lot of other people I always pretend it's an Olympic race where I'm representing Ireland. "Ireland takes an early lead—oh, here comes Germany! Ireland puts it into gear . . . Ireland pulls ahead . . . and Ireland wins!"

4.

wiped:

hygiene
heavy
and
contamination
control

I have the need to smell the dental floss each time I pull it out from between my teeth. Sometimes when other people are around I have to turn my back, in case they catch me sniffing the floss.

When I go to a public bathroom I touch
absolutely nothing and make sure I have
complete privacy. I ball up some paper, wet
it in the sink, scrub the toilet seat, and dry it
with another piece. Then I cover the gap
made between the door and the wall with
a long strip of toilet paper. When I have to
leave, I usually open the door with my foot.

I dislike wearing shoes. I will take mine off as soon as I can, and often walk around restaurants, stores, and even sidewalks barefoot. But I cannot for the life of me go into a public restroom without my shoes on.

I microwave my toothbrush after every use to kill germs that may have accumulated on it.

When I eat cereal
I can't pour the milk
straight from the carton
to my bowl: the fumes
from the bowl of cereal
would enter the milk jug
when air fills the poured
milk's space. Instead I
pour my milk into a glass,
then from the glass to the
cereal bowl.

Before I turn the shower off I have to wring out my hair the number of times equal to my age plus one. It makes birthdays really exciting.

I can't eat birthday cake on which people have blown out candles. We either hold their candles while the cake is presented, or we put them all in one corner and I eat the far end of the cake. I just know the birthday person's spit is going all over the cake and it's disgusting. Babies are the exception.

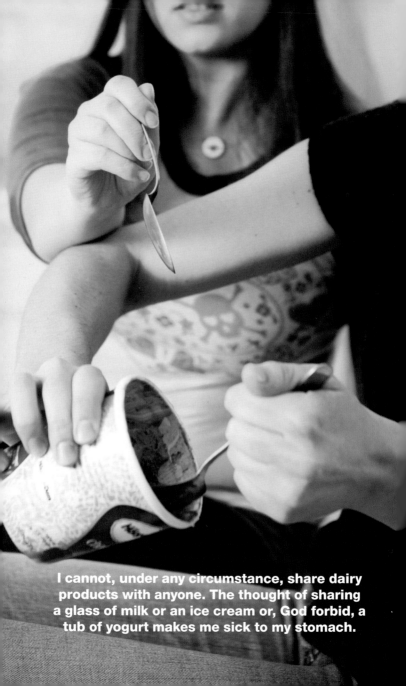

I cannot, under any circumstance, share dairy products with anyone. The thought of sharing a glass of milk or an ice cream or, God forbid, a tub of yogurt makes me sick to my stomach.

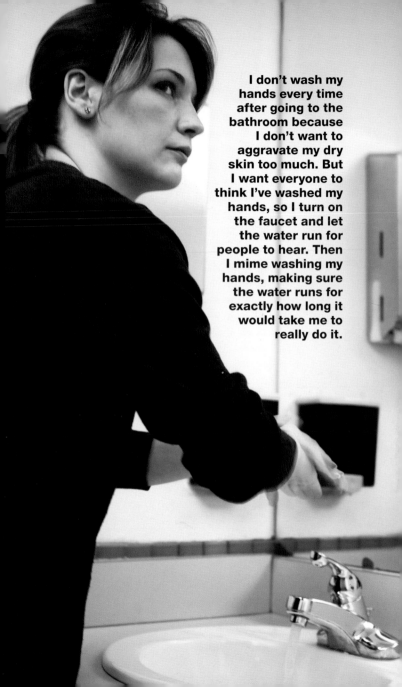

I don't wash my hands every time after going to the bathroom because I don't want to aggravate my dry skin too much. But I want everyone to think I've washed my hands, so I turn on the faucet and let the water run for people to hear. Then I mime washing my hands, making sure the water runs for exactly how long it would take me to really do it.

I hate tomatoes yet whenever I order a sandwich I deliberately order it with tomatoes and then pick them off. This way I keep what I call the "essence of tomato." I don't like sandwiches that don't have the essence.

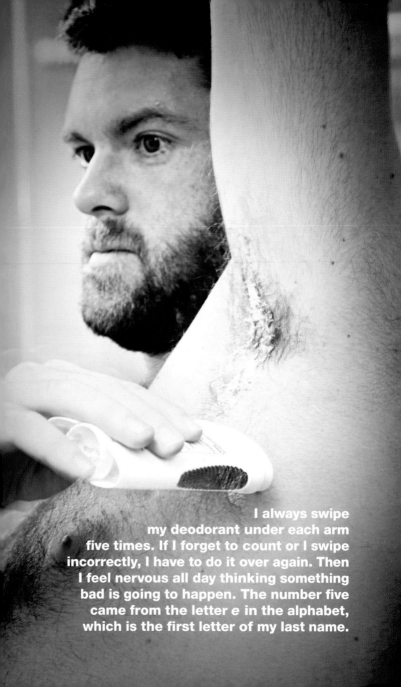

I always swipe my deodorant under each arm five times. If I forget to count or I swipe incorrectly, I have to do it over again. Then I feel nervous all day thinking something bad is going to happen. The number five came from the letter e in the alphabet, which is the first letter of my last name.

I have to eat Cheetos with chopsticks because I don't like the cheese getting stuck to my fingers.

Whenever I undress to take a shower I always put clothing from the lower half of my body on the floor, but I cannot do the same with items from the upper half of my body. I believe that the upper-half clothes are too clean to be thrown on the floor and the lower-half clothes are too dirty to be put on the counter.

I always have to burn any meat I eat. I am so worried I will smell that undercooked, moist essence.

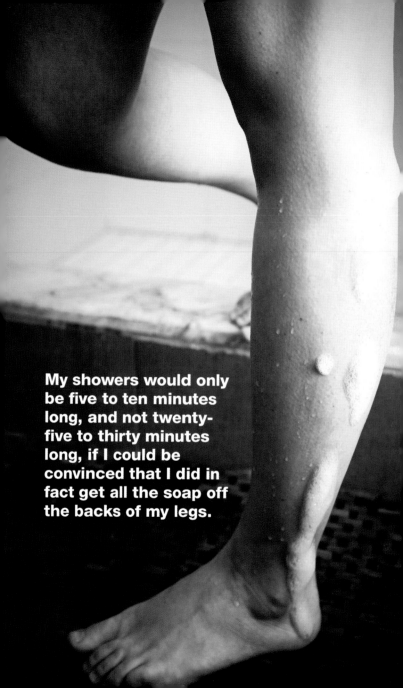

My showers would only be five to ten minutes long, and not twenty-five to thirty minutes long, if I could be convinced that I did in fact get all the soap off the backs of my legs.

When I'm wearing a skirt I have to subtly smooth my hand over my butt at least five times after I go to the bathroom to make sure the skirt's not tucked into my underwear.

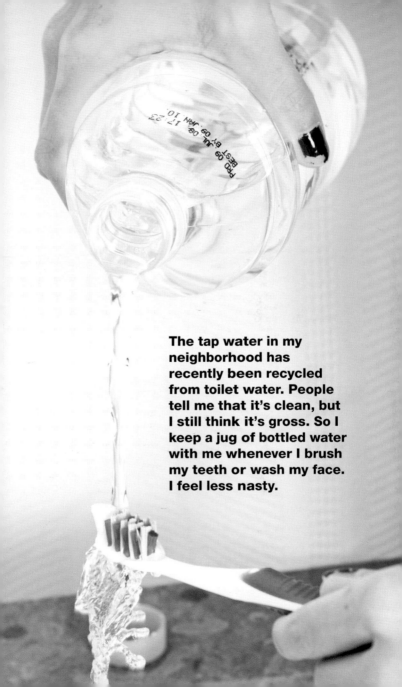

The tap water in my neighborhood has recently been recycled from toilet water. People tell me that it's clean, but I still think it's gross. So I keep a jug of bottled water with me whenever I brush my teeth or wash my face. I feel less nasty.

I can't bear to touch the handles of taps, so I turn them on and off with my elbows. Turning them off with my hands means I have to rewash them (starting a vicious cycle). I also have to flush the toilet with my feet—never with my hands.

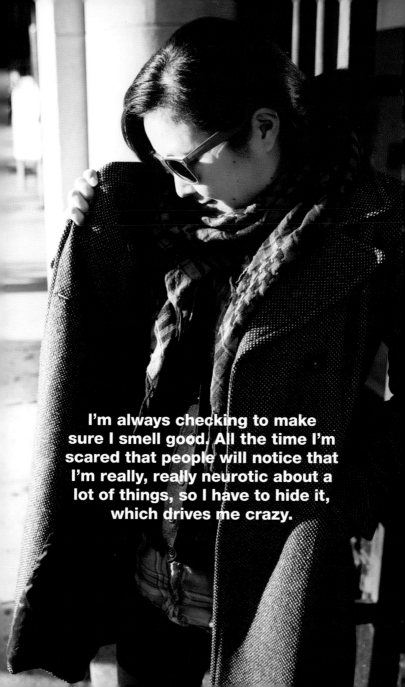

I'm always checking to make sure I smell good. All the time I'm scared that people will notice that I'm really, really neurotic about a lot of things, so I have to hide it, which drives me crazy.

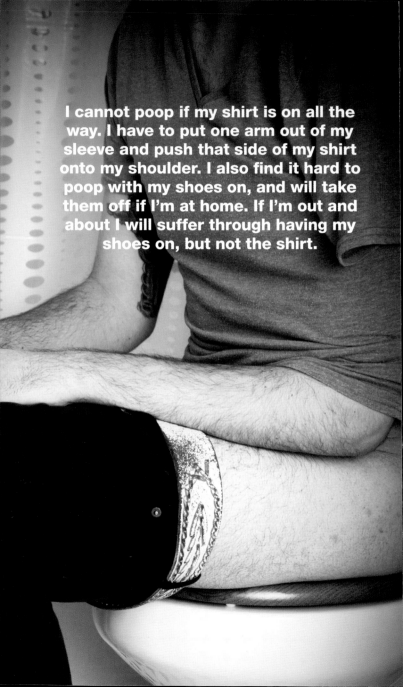

I cannot poop if my shirt is on all the way. I have to put one arm out of my sleeve and push that side of my shirt onto my shoulder. I also find it hard to poop with my shoes on, and will take them off if I'm at home. If I'm out and about I will suffer through having my shoes on, but not the shirt.

5.

law and order: the need for neatness

Everything on my desk or for school has to be color-coded. If I can't find colored items, I become quite frustrated and will dedicate unbelievable amounts of time and money to have all the supplies I need to organize something.

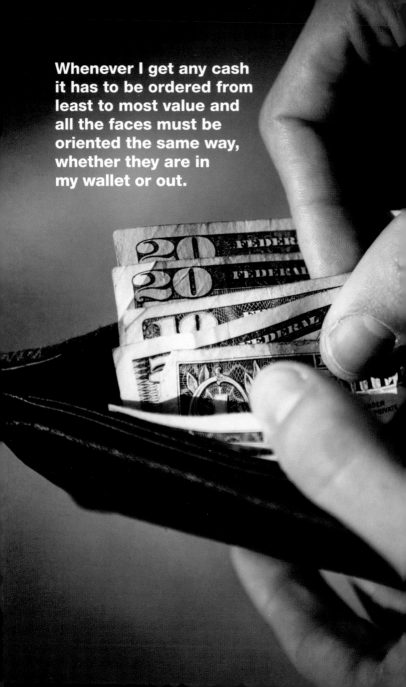

Whenever I get any cash it has to be ordered from least to most value and all the faces must be oriented the same way, whether they are in my wallet or out.

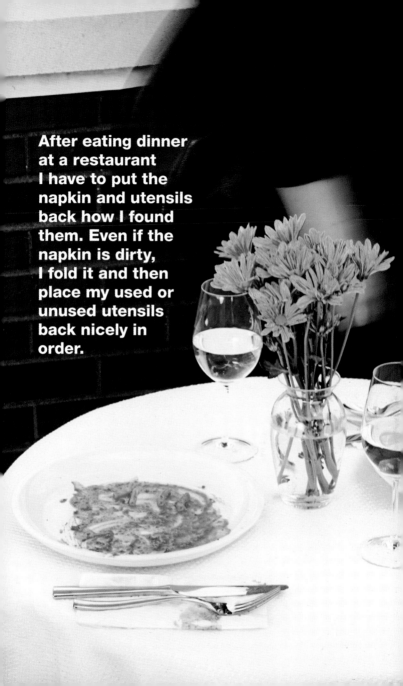

After eating dinner at a restaurant I have to put the napkin and utensils back how I found them. Even if the napkin is dirty, I fold it and then place my used or unused utensils back nicely in order.

I have to fold every piece of paper and plastic trash neatly into a small square, from plastic bags to tissues. It makes it look pretty.

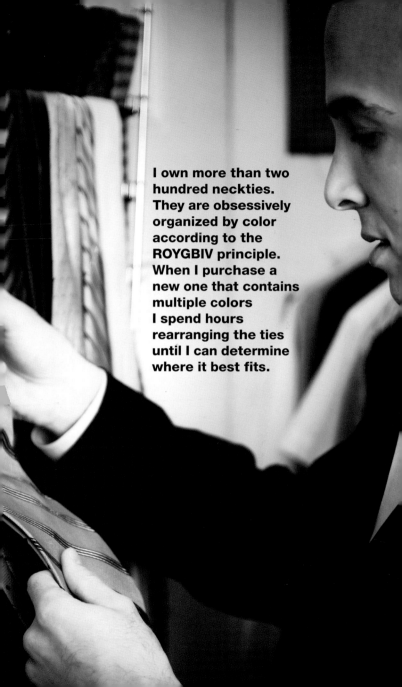

I own more than two hundred neckties. They are obsessively organized by color according to the ROYGBIV principle. When I purchase a new one that contains multiple colors I spend hours rearranging the ties until I can determine where it best fits.

When I eat colored sweets (Skittles, Smarties, etc.) I have to arrange them by color, then pull out enough of them to create a Fibonacci triangle before I can eat them (in ascending numerical order). Any excess sweets that do not fit the pattern have to be eaten in one go before I can start on the patterned sweets.

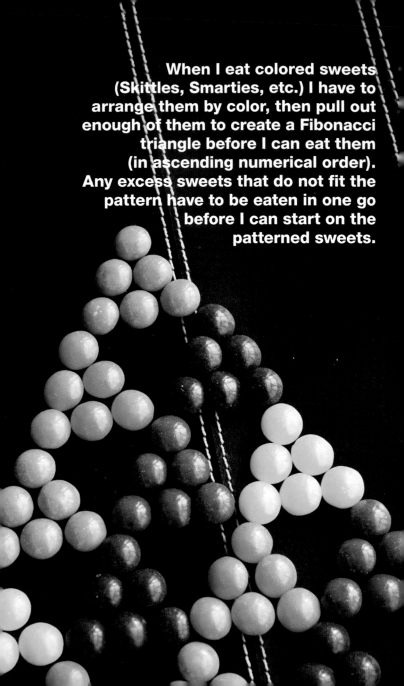

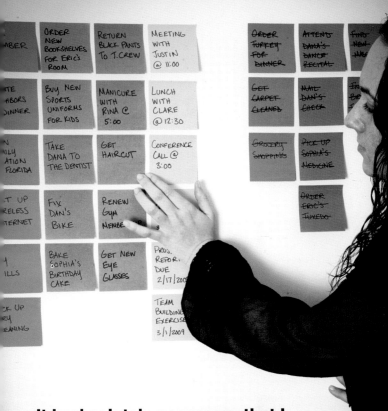

It is absolutely necessary that I write everything down on Post-it notes and paste them up on my reminder wall. I write Post-its for things that I've already completed. These are the best, because I get to write the note, and then immediately cross it out with a thick Sharpie, feeling productive as hell and ahead of the game.

My father saves French's Mustard bottles and reuses them for everything from barbecue sauce to shampoo. He has also cleaned, refilled, and reused the same hairspray bottle for approximately two years. He likes how that particular bottle sprays.

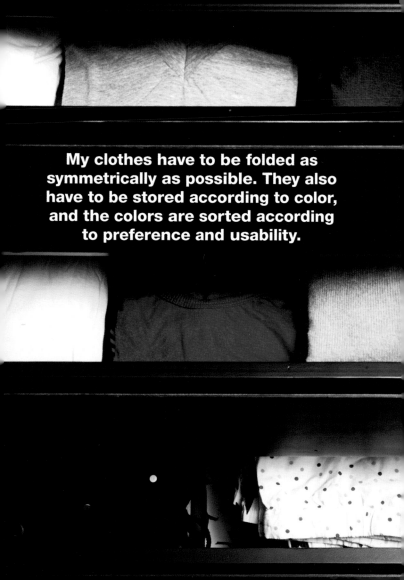

My clothes have to be folded as symmetrically as possible. They also have to be stored according to color, and the colors are sorted according to preference and usability.

**When wrapping presents I line up
the patterns on the wrapping paper
so that they match. I particularly
like stripes and plaids**

I like all of my canned foods to be in alphabetical order. The labels must all be facing forward and aligned perfectly so that I can see the front of the can.

Every night before I go to bed I have to place all the products I plan on using in the morning out on my bathroom counter, in the specific order I plan on using them. Every morning, after I have used each product, I place them back in the cabinet, thereby ensuring that my ritual will begin again that night.

Whenever I get a coffee from a coffee shop I have to turn the cardboard sleeve so that the logo on the sleeve matches the logo on the coffee cup.

If I see any colored objects, like tacks or markers, I have to put them in rainbow order. I did this with push pins at school during my junior year. Everyone in my class kept wondering who did it.

I trim all my candlewicks to exactly a quarter inch. Before lighting a candle, I must check its wick length. I like tight, calm, perfect little flames. A wildly blazing candle negates any notion of mood lighting and sends me into a frenzy of blowing out candles and then snipping the wicks so I can relax.

I can't relax if anything on a surface (desk, coffee table, etc.) is not at a right angle.

Around Christmas-time, when all the presents are under the tree, I have to constantly arrange them to look picture-perfect, like something you would see in a magazine. Then I take photographs until I get the perfect one. Last Christmas I got 168 photos!

My to-do lists must be written perfectly. If I mess up or don't feel satisfied with the quality of my handwriting, I will throw my to-do lists out and start over. Sometimes it takes me five or six times to get it right. Then once I cross a few items off the list, I have to rewrite it again

When I eat any cookie with cream in the middle I must pull it apart so that one cookie has all of the cream and one has none. I only eat the cookie with the cream, but I cannot eat the cookie at all if it doesn't pull apart the right way. I then stack the uneaten cookies and offer them to others or just throw them out.

I wear all black every day. I plan out my black outfits to perfection. Despite owning many different varieties of black clothes, everyone just says, "You're always in black." They never notice the variety of different black clothes I spend so much time putting together.

I end up spending my time at a department store aligning the hangers on which the clothes sit so that they are all evenly spaced along the rack.

At school, when our worksheets have blanks provided for our answers, my answer must fill up the whole blank. If not, I get very irritated.

5. What is meant by ___
Manifest destiny is the ___
as their right to ___

6. Name three Indian tribes.
• CHEROKEE
• IROQUOIS
• CHEYENNE

7. Why was the buffalo important to the Indians?

Each time I buy a Slurpee I try to make five perfectly even stripes of flavor in the cup. The cup must be clear—one size down from largest—and the chosen colors must complement one another in flavor and, most important, in color. I choose a straw color to complement the beverage.

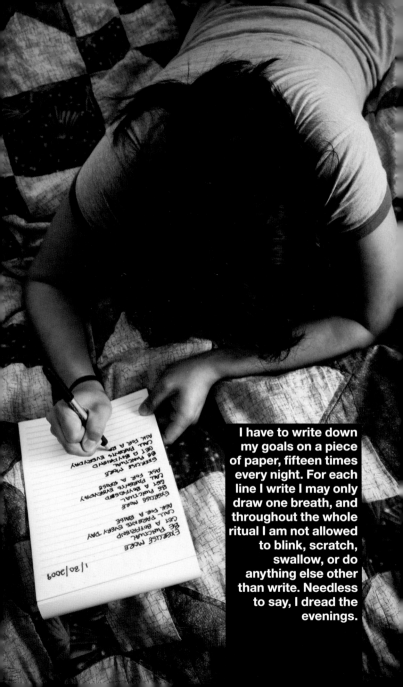

I have to write down my goals on a piece of paper, fifteen times every night. For each line I write I may only draw one breath, and throughout the whole ritual I am not allowed to blink, scratch, swallow, or do anything else other than write. Needless to say, I dread the evenings.

I arrange colors, like in a box of crayons,
in a heat scale (red is hot and blue is cold).
If they end up out of order, it drives me crazy
until they are put back in the right order.

neurotic or else:

beware of the consequences

Every time I go into the bathroom,
I have to punch the shower curtain.
I am afraid that someone is hiding in
the shower, so I try to get a low blow in
before their attack. On two occasions
I have knocked the curtain rod off the
wall and have had to confess to my
host why and how it happened.

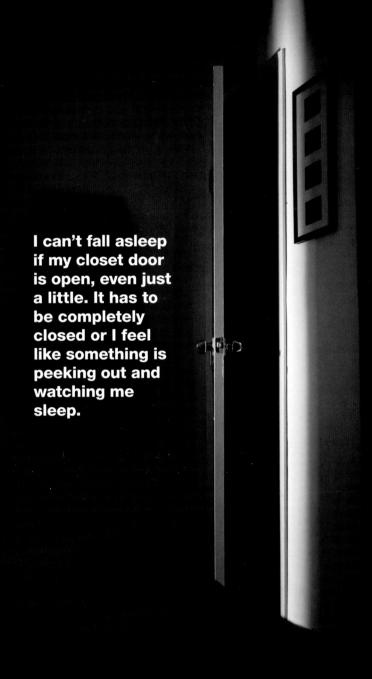

I can't fall asleep if my closet door is open, even just a little. It has to be completely closed or I feel like something is peeking out and watching me sleep.

Whenever I am about to go through a revolving door I take as big a breath as I can and hold it, because the person who just came through before me might have farted in there and I would be trapped with it if the door got stuck.

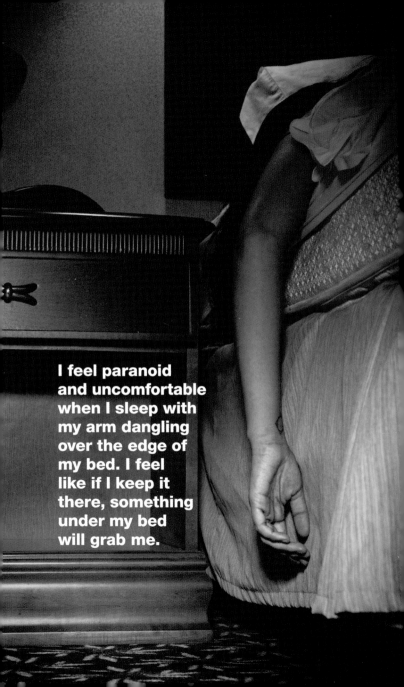

I feel paranoid and uncomfortable when I sleep with my arm dangling over the edge of my bed. I feel like if I keep it there, something under my bed will grab me.

I cannot eat around any males at all, including family members. I cannot bring myself to eat around them. I just stop.

When I was little I thought I was being followed by a hidden camera crew. It made me very paranoid when I was doing something bad, even if I was completely alone. Once I hid under my bed to eat a cookie I had stolen so the camera people wouldn't see.

I wake up three to four times a night to make sure my alarm clock is set.

I am always paranoid that I forgot to set it and I will wake up late.

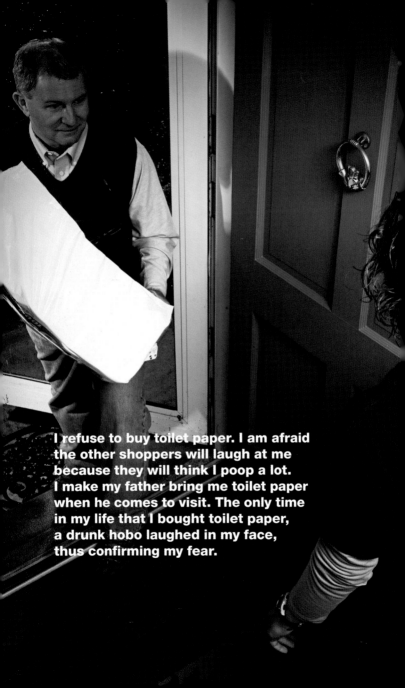

I refuse to buy toilet paper. I am afraid the other shoppers will laugh at me because they will think I poop a lot. I make my father bring me toilet paper when he comes to visit. The only time in my life that I bought toilet paper, a drunk hobo laughed in my face, thus confirming my fear.

Every time I unroll one of those Pillsbury Biscuits cans I do it while holding it as far away from me as possible because I feel like it is going to explode and injure me.

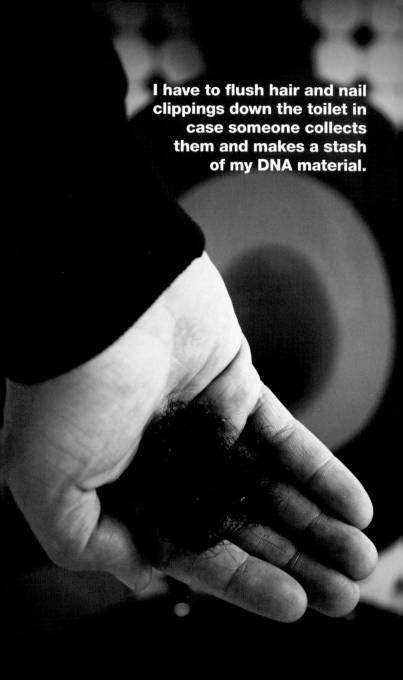

I have to flush hair and nail clippings down the toilet in case someone collects them and makes a stash of my DNA material.

Whenever I finish using my webcam, I have to cover it with a piece of paper in case someone hacks into my computer and uses it to look at me.

I can't be in an overorganized
space. If something's not out of place,
I mess up one thing—even if it's just moving
a magazine off a pile. If it's all too flawless,
I'm afraid I'm in some sort of mix between
The Truman Show and *The Stepford Wives*.

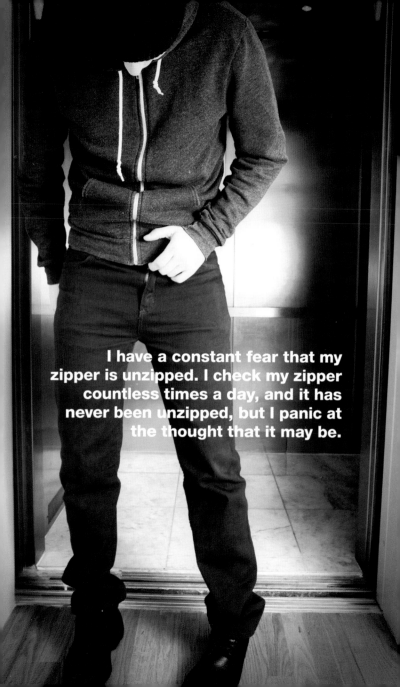

I have a constant fear that my zipper is unzipped. I check my zipper countless times a day, and it has never been unzipped, but I panic at the thought that it may be.

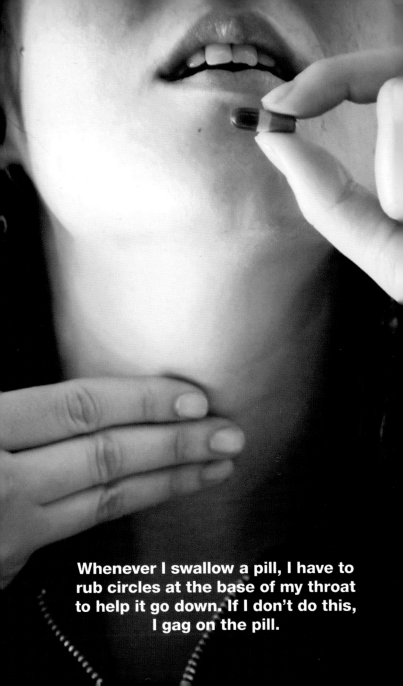

Whenever I swallow a pill, I have to rub circles at the base of my throat to help it go down. If I don't do this, I gag on the pill.

I absolutely must bite my straws when I drink out of them. It makes me feel in control of the amount of liquid that I am drinking. If I drink out of the straw without biting it, I feel like I'm going to drown.

Whenever I babysit and the family owns a cat, I do absolutely nothing out of the ordinary (refusing to use the restroom, eat or drink anything, or watch TV), because I just know that the animal will detail everything I did to the parents when they return.

When I use tampons I'm always afraid I might accidentally insert two tampons in a row. Just thinking about it makes me sick. I have to write "Don't forget to take out your tampon" on each tampon wrapper to remind myself to take out the previous tampon. My stomach aches for fear that I might have put in two tampons in a row.

I have a fear of burning down my house with my hair straightener. I usually forget that I unplugged it. Sometimes I'll do a silly dance or odd motion after I've unplugged it, so that if I don't remember unplugging it, I'll definitely remember the dance.

My coworker thinks she has mad cow disease. She will stand up, close her eyes, stretch out her arms, and touch her nose with her index fingers over and over. Next, she will balance on one foot then the other to assure herself that the disease hasn't progressed.

Whenever I'm drinking around my computer I have this heart-stopping visual of the drink spilling all over my keyboard and ruining it, with the computer smoking, popping, and short-circuiting. This visual is so scary that I have to make sure that the drink is far enough away from the computer so that even it if spills, the splash won't reach my computer.

Whenever someone holds open a door for me I must touch the door to make sure it will not suddenly slam shut and squish me. Just a fingertip will do, although this causes a major inconvenience when there are people between me and the door.

When my goldfish died I somehow got it into my head that my mom had not flushed it down the toilet like she had said, but instead had slipped it into my strawberry milk. I checked for a dead goldfish in my milk every morning for about two years.

When I mail letters I must open
the mailbox door at least three
times to be sure my letters went
down. I am paranoid that my
mail will get stuck on the slide,
and when the next person opens
the mailbox door, my letters will
go flying out into the abyss.

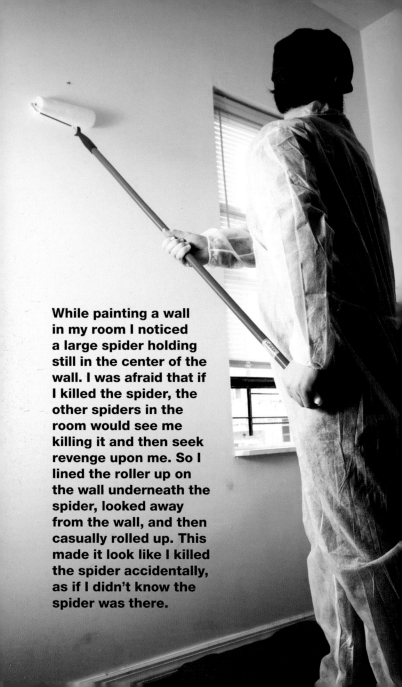

While painting a wall in my room I noticed a large spider holding still in the center of the wall. I was afraid that if I killed the spider, the other spiders in the room would see me killing it and then seek revenge upon me. So I lined the roller up on the wall underneath the spider, looked away from the wall, and then casually rolled up. This made it look like I killed the spider accidentally, as if I didn't know the spider was there.

My ears have to be covered at all times. I cover them with my hair or headphones or blankets and pillows when I sleep. I fear that bugs will crawl into my ears if they are exposed.

7.

relish-worthy:
savor, rinse, repeat

Whenever I buy a new book
I have to bury my nose in between
a few random pages and take in
a deep breath.

When I spread anything on a piece of bread or muffin I am compelled to spread that substance over the entire space of the bread, all the way to the edge, and up into the corners. Every single bit of space must be covered.

Whenever my dad would get me an ice cream cone he would eat the twirl before he handed it to me. Now I have to eat the twirl right away so no one else can, even if I'm alone.

When eating chips I check each one to see which side has more flavor. Then I make sure that side ends up facedown on my tongue to maximize my chip-eating pleasure.

It's hard for me to go past the railing in my house without pretending my hand is a roller coaster, putting my eyes level with it, and making appropriate zoom sounds.

Whenever I eat waffles every single hole has to have syrup in it or I will not eat it. If I'm already eating and notice one hole is missing syrup, I can't finish the waffle.

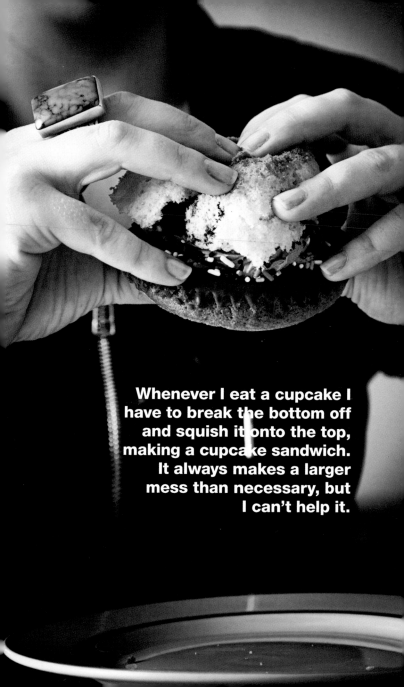

Whenever I eat a cupcake I have to break the bottom off and squish it onto the top, making a cupcake sandwich. It always makes a larger mess than necessary, but I can't help it.

Every time I blow my
nose I have to see
what's in the tissue.

I cannot drink a glass of chocolate milk unless I have a spoon and slurp it down a spoonful at a time. If the chocolate milk is in a carton, I will transfer it to a glass and proceed as normal. Regular milk and all other drinks are fine sans spoon.

Every time I open a new package of food I have to smell it or else I become really uncomfortable. It is especially necessary when I open a new pack of gum. I try to do it as discreetly as possible so people don't see me.

When I eat a Snickers bar I have to eat the nougat off the bottom first, then nibble and suck the chocolate off, then suck the caramel off the caramel-covered peanuts, and, finally, chew the peanuts. I do this in one-inch increments down the length of the bar. I only eat them at the movies so no one will know.

I have to squish my
sandwich flat before I eat it.

I have to eat ice cream
with a fork. I just have to,
or no ice cream.

I used to make little cakes of food on my fork—I would have a bottom layer of rice, then a piece of lettuce, then a carrot, then a piece of chicken. Creating the layers would make me the last person at the dinner table pretty much every day. I don't do it anymore. Well, not as often.

8.

zen
and
the
art
of
process:
the
religion
of
rituals

When stirring sugar into coffee I must clink the spoon once per rotation, and I must do this ten times per spoon of sugar added to the coffee. The coffee must also still be swirling before I can add the milk.

My girlfriend has to say
"Ilco" before she opens the
front door with her house key.
The name on the key is Ilco.
I caught her whispering it once,
and she confessed!

Whenever I read a magazine I underline or cross out the text as I read it. I have to use a fine-point Pilot Precise V5/7 Rolling Ball pen (not extra fine). I mark the magazine in different patterns. The more I do it, the more new ways I discover to cross things out.

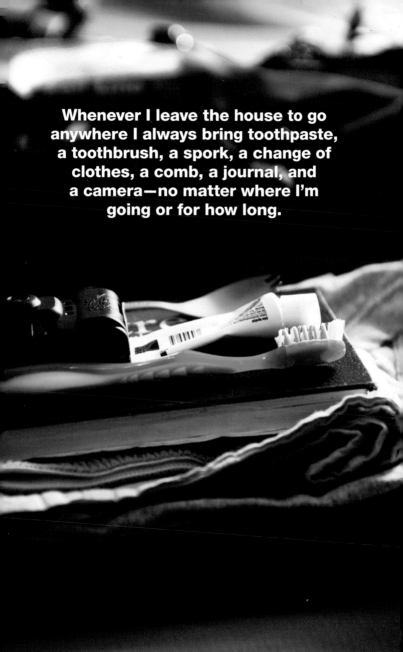

Whenever I leave the house to go anywhere I always bring toothpaste, a toothbrush, a spork, a change of clothes, a comb, a journal, and a camera—no matter where I'm going or for how long.

I can only eat jelly doughnuts
by squeezing all the jelly out.

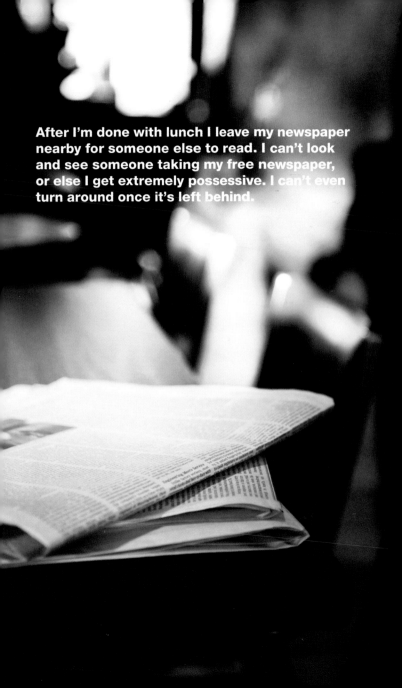

After I'm done with lunch I leave my newspaper nearby for someone else to read. I can't look and see someone taking my free newspaper, or else I get extremely possessive. I can't even turn around once it's left behind.

**When I eat macaroni and cheese—
or any pasta with holes—I have to poke
my fork through the holes and eat them
four at a time. Yes, it takes forever!**

I hoard subscription cards from magazines, fill out bogus addresses on them, and drop them in the mail. Sometimes I hoard them for months until I have a huge pile and mail them all at once.

When I eat a Hershey's Kiss
I have to bite off the point at the top.
I don't really know why, but I've
been eating them that way forever.

Whenever I drink something cold enough to leave water rings where it sits I always have to move the glass/can/bottle so that a new ring is created, but it still must overlap with the other rings. This leads to a large series of expansive Olympics-type ring designs.

I open the mailbox every time I walk by. Even when I know there is no mail, like on Sundays or at 3:00

in the morning. Depending on how often I walk out-side, I will check the mailbox several times a day.

I cut the tops off peppers, remove the cores, then cut vertical slices following the lines of rotational symmetry. Not only do I believe this to be mathematically the best way to cut a pepper, I will actively shout at anybody I see not following this method—they're doing it all wrong.

I mark the days off of my calendar every night with a black Sharpie, and I always have to smell the marker. If someone is watching me, I try to do it discreetly so the other person won't notice.

If I wake up at any time during the night, I have to eat a granola bar. Otherwise I can't fall back asleep. I always have boxes and boxes of granola bars in my kitchen.

When I cook something that requires pepper I have to turn the grinder a number of times equal to my age. My food will get hotter as I get older.

I live alone, so I don't shop for groceries very often. Sometimes I keep spoiled food in the fridge for a while so it doesn't look empty.

When I leave my house I have to make sure both of my dogs are in sight. If one is not, I have to find it and move it to where I can see both dogs at the same time. This is to avoid the fear of having left them outside.

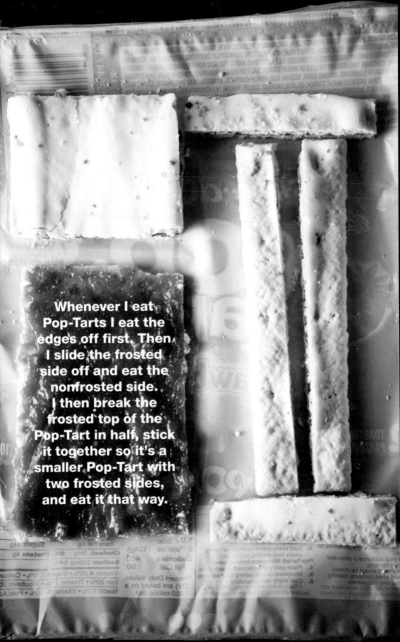

Whenever I eat Pop-Tarts I eat the edges off first. Then I slide the frosted side off and eat the nonfrosted side. I then break the frosted top of the Pop-Tart in half, stick it together so it's a smaller Pop-Tart with two frosted sides, and eat it that way.

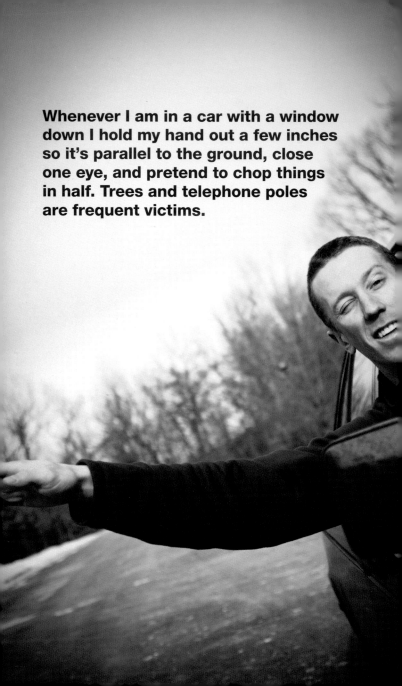

Whenever I am in a car with a window down I hold my hand out a few inches so it's parallel to the ground, close one eye, and pretend to chop things in half. Trees and telephone poles are frequent victims.

When I was little I had to put ice in my hot soup. Sometimes I put too many ice cubes in and the soup got cold, so I'd heat it up, and if it got too hot, I'd add ice again. I'd never wait for it to cool down naturally.

When I eat Smarties I have to know
what color the candy is before I eat it.
If I forget to check before it goes into
my mouth, I have to take it out and look.

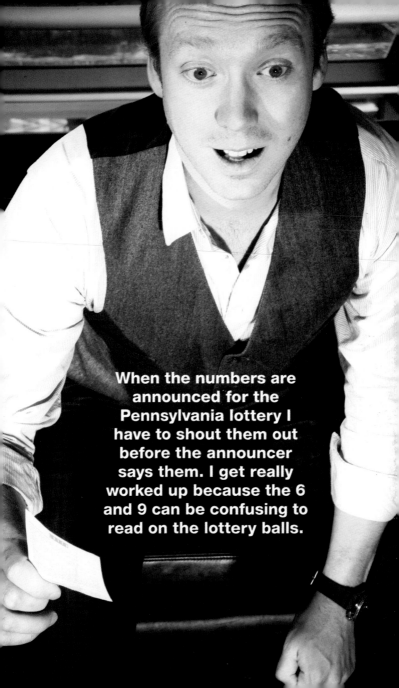

When the numbers are announced for the Pennsylvania lottery I have to shout them out before the announcer says them. I get really worked up because the 6 and 9 can be confusing to read on the lottery balls.

When I'm shopping I will never buy the first product. I always get the third or fourth one behind the first. I feel like the first product was touched, and I don't want it.

I have to eat my corn on the cob one row at a time, making sure to get the entire kernel off the cob. Interestingly, my best friend also does the same thing.

**When I'm using my BlackBerry
I have to make sure the top left icon is
selected before turning it off, putting it
in my pocket, or locking the key pad.**

When eating a sandwich,
especially a peanut butter and jelly sandwich,
I prefer to eat the crust off first and then continue
eating in a circle. That way the filling of the
sandwich gets pushed toward the middle, making
the last few bites especially good.

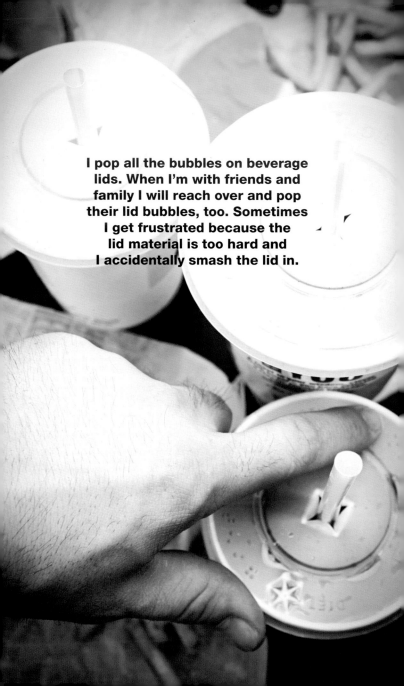

I pop all the bubbles on beverage lids. When I'm with friends and family I will reach over and pop their lid bubbles, too. Sometimes I get frustrated because the lid material is too hard and I accidentally smash the lid in.

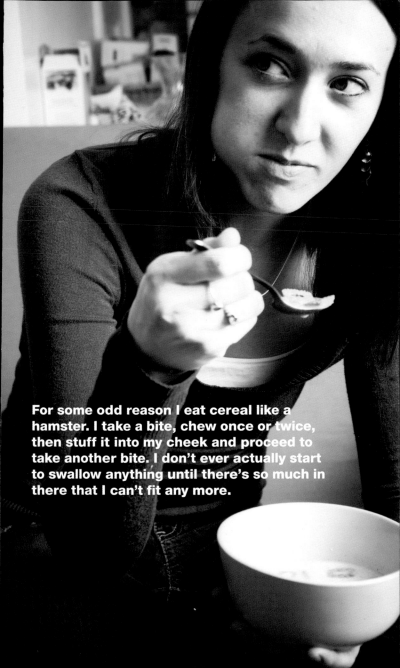

For some odd reason I eat cereal like a hamster. I take a bite, chew once or twice, then stuff it into my cheek and proceed to take another bite. I don't ever actually start to swallow anything until there's so much in there that I can't fit any more.

When I buy dinner at a restaurant I always leave a tip so that the total is a palindrome.

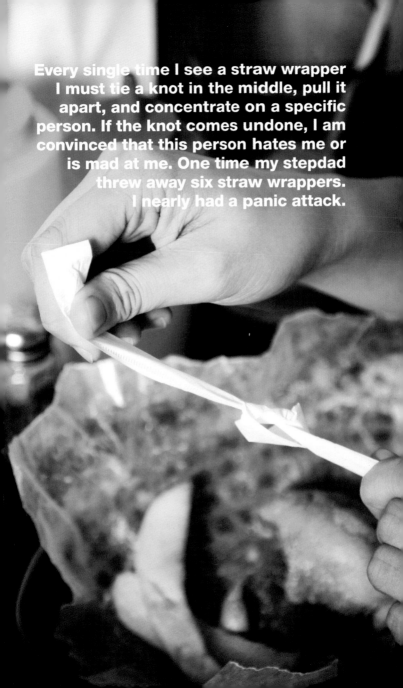

Every single time I see a straw wrapper I must tie a knot in the middle, pull it apart, and concentrate on a specific person. If the knot comes undone, I am convinced that this person hates me or is mad at me. One time my stepdad threw away six straw wrappers. I nearly had a panic attack.

When I pass baked goods in the grocery I have to squeeze them. Entenmann's frustrates the hell out of me, because the box is too stiff and the plastic window will rip with a loud popping noise if I poke it too hard.

9.

jedi mind tricks:
micromanaging the supernatural

I always pretend I have superpowers. When I am in an elevator I wave my hands as if I am making the door open and close, and the elevator go up and down. Same goes for automatic doors and car windows.

When my beard gets too long I feel I have itchy evil hairs. I will try to pull these hairs out, but I usually miss. If I do pull one out, and the itching stops, I feel much better. Then I'm forced to bite that evil beard hair to punish it for causing me discomfort.

Whenever I see a penny I have to pick it up. Otherwise I think I'm going to have bad luck all day. Even if the penny is sitting in something gross. I'll nudge it out with my foot and find a way to pick it up. I have a lot of pennies.

I have an issue with the eggs in my refrigerator. My roommates take eggs out of the carton willy-nilly, without any thought as to evenness. So every time someone eats an egg, I have to arrange them so that each one has a partner. If there is one lonely egg, I either eat it or throw it away to put it out of its misery.

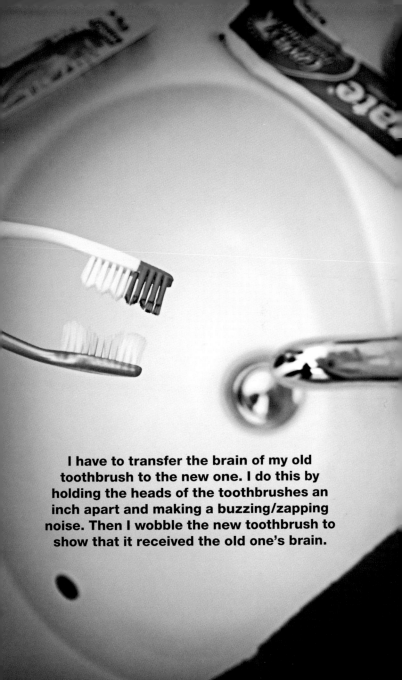

I have to transfer the brain of my old toothbrush to the new one. I do this by holding the heads of the toothbrushes an inch apart and making a buzzing/zapping noise. Then I wobble the new toothbrush to show that it received the old one's brain.

I have to put every single ingredient into small custard bowls before cooking. I then address a make-believe audience as if I am on a cooking show, telling them every step it takes to make the dish I am preparing. I even do it with things like boxed macaroni and cheese or cake mix. If I don't do it, I think the food tastes funny or is improperly made.

I flip a quarter to do most of my decision making, from should I go out tonight to should I quit my job. I always trust in the quarter, for I believe if you do, it will give you accurate answers. I think if I don't obey the quarter, something bad could happen.

I always felt that unless I arranged the cups in the cupboard very neatly in even rows, then something horrible would happen (i.e., a friend would die) or I would miss some magical event because I had thrown off the will of the universe.

When I leave my apartment
I take a very close look at
the first few people I see for
signs of zombification or
a look of horror like there
might be zombies nearby.

which

fects of t

headache

belief als

I can't handle hearing or seeing the word *headache* without fear of getting a headache myself. Sometimes, like now, I can reason my way out of it, but other times, it will make me so paranoid that I end up getting a headache because of it. Man, I hate headaches.

I am twenty years old, and I have just one stuffed animal. I cannot stand it if she is on the floor or upside down, because I don't want her to be uncomfortable! I feel terrible packing her in a suitcase, so I put her between clothes so she is more comfortable and not squished against the sides.

I have to stroke the spine of every book I read. If the spine is broken, I will not read it. Instead I give it a quiet funeral in the garden. It is a very somber affair.

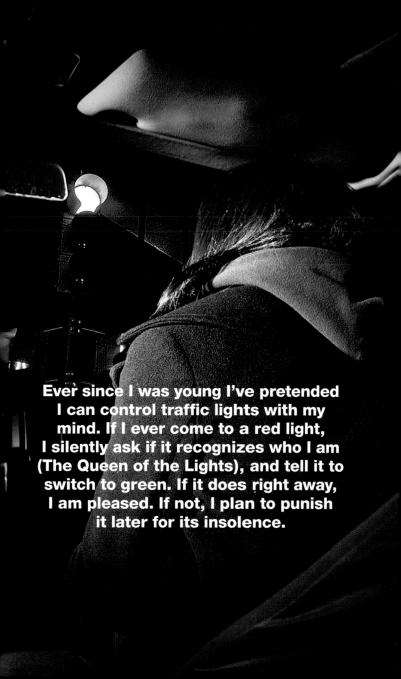

Ever since I was young I've pretended I can control traffic lights with my mind. If I ever come to a red light, I silently ask if it recognizes who I am (The Queen of the Lights), and tell it to switch to green. If it does right away, I am pleased. If not, I plan to punish it later for its insolence.

When I see a dented package
or a can with a torn label I'll buy it because
I feel sorry for it. When I'm feeling especially
charitable I'll go for a bruised apple.

When I'm in an
unfamiliar place
I have to touch
everything in sight
so I can have a tactile
memory of the place,
just in case I go blind
one day.

Whenever I walk up the basement stairs I have a quick pretend gunfight with an imaginary person running out from behind the wall. I shoot him so he stays down there.

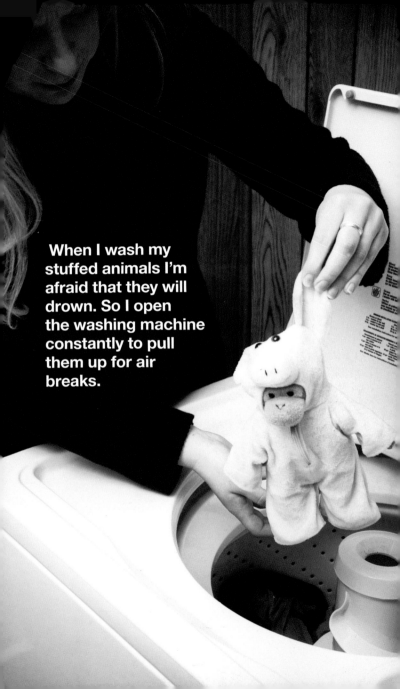

When I wash my stuffed animals I'm afraid that they will drown. So I open the washing machine constantly to pull them up for air breaks.

I can only get on a bicycle
from the left side because as
a child I always pretended my
bike was a horse, and a horse
is mounted from the left side.

I only eat fortune cookies that pop when I squeeze them. This is my method of making certain that the fortune contained within is in fact mine and that the cosmic repercussions of my reading said fortune will also take place.

My friend always punches the roof of the car whenever we drive through a yellow light, over train tracks, or past a cemetery. It is the most distracting thing for a driver. I'll hear the *wham* and see her jerk in my peripheral vision, which makes me think we've been hit.

I used to have a fear of touching
globes. The rationale was that by
touching a globe I would destroy the
actual country under my fingertips
and cause millions of deaths.
Not very logical, I guess.

When I was younger I had a strange belief that inanimate objects have feelings. If I ate a piece of candy, I would have to eat another so that I could throw two wrappers away so they wouldn't be lonely.

Whenever I'm intimate with someone
I always have to take down the pictures
of my family or lay them facedown
because I feel like that person can
see everything I'm doing.

10.

and other neurotic flavors

Whenever I bowl I must pretend
that I am a British announcer talking
aloud about my impending strike.
If I don't, I get a gutter ball every time.

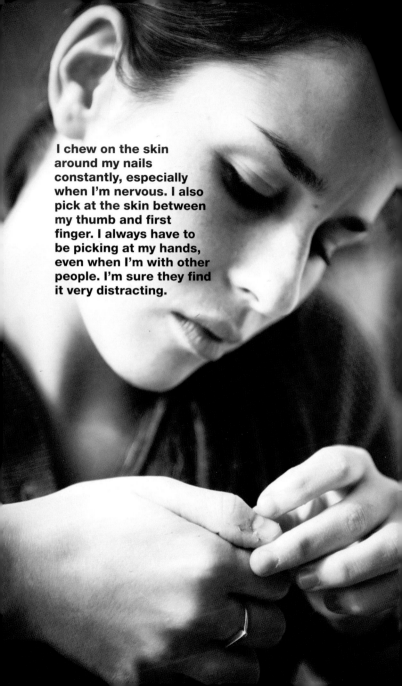

I chew on the skin around my nails constantly, especially when I'm nervous. I also pick at the skin between my thumb and first finger. I always have to be picking at my hands, even when I'm with other people. I'm sure they find it very distracting.

Whenever I take my shoes and socks off I can't help but use my big toe to point at objects in my room. Sometimes it is difficult to situate my body to make this happen, but I feel more comfortable once the correct vector is achieved.

I can't allow my husband to go grocery shopping with me because whenever we get to the salad dressing aisle he has to shake each bottle whose solid contents have settled to the bottom. I don't keep Italian or oil-based salad dressings in the house because my husband will shake them each time he opens the refrigerator. Sometimes I suspect he goes to the fridge for that purpose and no other.

.. / .... .- ...- . / - .... / .-. . .- .-.. .-.. -.-- /
.-. -. -. ---- .-- .. -. --. / .- -.. -.. .-. -.-. - .. --- -.
/ - --- / - -.-- .--. .. -. --. / -- --- .-. ... .
.-.-.- / .... . .-.. .--. / -- . / .--. .-.. . .- ... . !

**[I have this really annoying addiction
to typing in Morse. Help me, please!]**

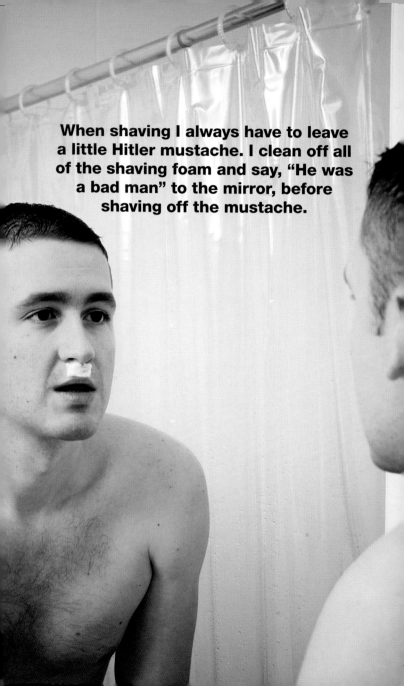

When shaving I always have to leave a little Hitler mustache. I clean off all of the shaving foam and say, "He was a bad man" to the mirror, before shaving off the mustache.

When I walk over a bridge I have to hold on really tight to my belongings because I fear I might throw them off.

Whenever I clean the lint trap in my dryer I have to sort through the lint to see if I can identify which articles of clothing it came from.

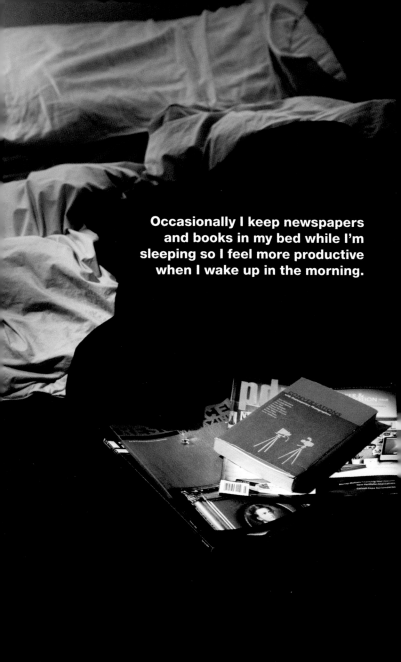

Occasionally I keep newspapers and books in my bed while I'm sleeping so I feel more productive when I wake up in the morning.

I am afraid of abbreviating in text messages, especially *tom* for *tomorrow*, even though I don't know any Toms. I came clean about this to the person I text the most. She laughed at me and told me it was okay to use *tom* for *tomorrow*. I still can't do it.

I can't drink the last bit of anything or finish off the bottle. By the end of one day I've accumulated a few Diet Coke bottles with about a quarter of the liquid sitting in the bottom. No matter how thirsty I am I have to open a new Coke or a fresh jug of milk.

I don't like blank space in my planner.
I go back and write in events that have passed
if I didn't write them in when they happened.
When I don't have concrete plans I write in
hobbies, movies, general hanging out,
brainstorming, even Tumblring (my blog).

I try to save every cap
to every beer that is drunk
in my presence (I even ask
bartenders to give me the
caps to the beers I drink at
the pub). Once they all fell
out of my pocket, and I had
to explain to a police officer
that I had not consumed
thirty-plus beers
that night.

When taking a standardized test with a separate answer sheet I will often go against my better judgment and change an answer if, say, there are too many *c*'s. I also get a lot of joy if I fill in *a* through *d* in order as answers.

When I walk down the meat aisle at the supermarket I feel an almost uncontrollable urge to slap the roast beefs. They're just so plump and round and shiny in their plastic wrap. Just one nice smack on the rump and I can go on with my day.

acknowledgments

■ I am certain that this book brought out my most neurotic behavior, making me both a joy and a nightmare to work with, but in either case, I am eternally grateful for all the unconditional support and help I received while putting together this book. I would like to thank:

Meg Thompson and Jud Laghi for finding the blog and having the vision to imagine it as a book.

Julia Cheiffetz, Sarah Burningham, and Katie Salisbury for their unwavering enthusiasm and guidance throughout the process.

Matthew Stacey for taking on the daunting task of photographing more than two hundred neuroses; Clare Seabright and Heami Lee for their assistance with the photography; and Meagan Stacey for her words of encouragement and for introducing me to Matthew at the start of the project.

Stephanie Judge, Dan Ramage, and Michael Kelly for all their stellar work on iamneurotic.com.

Sharon Rosenfeld, Rebecca Shulman, and Brian Chiger for not only helping me with the organization and development of the content, but also for holding my hand through all my own neuroses.

acknowledgments

All my amazing and generous friends for acting as models in the photos in this book:

Sophia Balakian, Christine Bang, Doug Bisson, Monet Brewerton, Brittany Bricen, Colleen Carroll, Derlen Chiu, Ben Coffey, Michael Don, Holly Eng, Shereen Escovitz, James Fedolfi, Tommy Fisher, Lizzie Flamenbaum, Mark Forscher, Lucas Fortier, Ashley Friedman, Dana Friedman, Joshua Gross, Katie Helke, Tommy Hernandez, Joyce Huang, Jeff Infantino, Rich Juzwiak (and Winston), Katy Knouf, David Kushner, Odelia Lee, Amy Levesque, Maggie Levin, Steve Listwon, Brianna Lloyd, Lisa Miao, Rose Napolitano, Erin Nelligan, Neil Orfield, Janene Podesta, Will Reuter, Ellie Roesch, Elian Rosenfeld, Justin Schneider, Liz Taing, Elise Tosun, Marisol Trowbridge, Alyssa Tsukushi, Jessica Varat, Catherine Walton, Jason Wells, Jenny Wong, and Eric Zwick.

And finally, a very special thanks to my fellow neurotics, whose contributions to the website are the reason why this book exists. The world would be a dull place without you and your neuroses. I am forever grateful and cannot thank you enough for sharing your neuroses.

Lianna Kong graduated from Wellesley College with a degree in Economics and French. She prints T-shirts and bakes pies in her spare time. She feels very secure in her neuroses.

Matthew Stacey is a photographer in New York City. You can see his work at www.matthewstacey.com.